Time for

Story and Pictures by
Joan Elizabeth Goodman

A GOLDEN BOOK • NEW YORK
Western Publishing Company, Inc., Racine, Wisconsin 53404

The sun had set. The moon was new in the sky.
"It's bedtime," Mama Skunk called to her kittens.
"Time to get ready for bed," said Papa Skunk.
"I don't want to," said Turnip. But no one
heard him.

Petunia, Mint, Chive, and Violet lined up at the bathroom sink. They brushed their teeth and washed their whiskers.

Turnip was last in line. He brushed each tooth, up and down, back and forth. Then he made a soapy beard and mustache.

"Hurry up!" called Mama. "Come to bed!"

Turnip inched down the hall, tracing the wallpaper vines with his paw. Very slowly he crawled into bed next to Violet.

Papa told his kittens a funny story. Then Mama sang a lullaby. All the kittens snuggled under their covers, yawned a last yawn, and closed their eyes.

Mama and Papa kissed them each good night and tiptoed out of the room.

Turnip was wide awake, listening to his brother and sisters sleeping. Violet nestled against his side.

"Honey buns, ice cream, yum-yum," she murmured in her sleep.

"Oh, no," thought Turnip.

"Yum-yum, gumdrops, crumb cakes, caramels," droned Violet.

Turnip climbed out of bed and padded down to the living room.

Papa was settled in his reading chair. Mama was busy folding laundry.

"Violet is talking about food in my ear," said Turnip.
"I can't go to sleep."

"Get in on the other side, next to Chive," said
Mama. "Then you won't hear her."

"I don't like Chive's side," said Turnip.

"Try it," said Papa.

So Turnip went back upstairs and got into bed next to Chive. He curled up into a tight little ball and listened. Sure enough, he could hardly hear Violet. Turnip closed his eyes and floated off into sleep.

FWOP! THUMP! Turnip found himself on the floor!
He got up and marched downstairs.

"Chive kicked me!" he said.
"I'm sure he didn't mean to," said Mama.
"But he kicked me out of bed!" said Turnip.
"Get in between Petunia and Mint," said Papa.

"Do I have to?" asked Turnip.

"Yes," said Mama. She led him back up to bed. Turnip squeezed into the middle.

"Sweet dreams, sweet one," said Mama, and she slipped out of the room.

It was awfully stuffy between Mint and Petunia.
Turnip tried lying first this way, then that. They were
closing in on him. Mint's breathing was growing into a
wheezy snore. Turnip turned away from her, onto the
Petunia side of his pillow.

It was slipping away! In her sleep Petunia was taking
his pillow!

Turnip leapt out of bed and flew down the stairs.

"They're squishing me! Mint is snoring, and Petunia *grabbed* my pillow!"

"There, there," said Mama. "You're such a tired kitten."

"I'm mad," said Turnip.

"It's very late," said Papa. "And time for everyone to be in bed."

Mama got Turnip a fresh pillow and turned out the lights. Papa carried Turnip piggyback upstairs and put him into bed next to Violet.

"But..." said Turnip.

"No buts," said Mama. "Just close your eyes."

They kissed Turnip and went to sleep in their own bedroom.

Soon after they'd left, Violet started in. "Yummy gumdrops, crumb cake, cream puffs..."

"I can't sleep here!" said Turnip.

He grabbed his pillow and went out into the hall. The house was dark and still.

"I'd like to sleep with Mama and Papa," thought Turnip. "But there isn't room in their bed, either."

He wandered into the bathroom. The bathtub was
just the right size for a bed. Turnip crawled into it with
his pillow, and two towels for covers.

"This is a good bed," Turnip said. He closed his eyes
and sighed.

Drip, drip, drop, drip. The faucet was leaking.
Turnip tried covering his ears.
DRIP, DRIP, DROP, DRIP! It was louder than
Violet. The tub was cold, too, and very hard. Turnip
climbed out and headed for the living room.

There was the laundry basket!

"The perfect bed!" Turnip said. He burrowed into the pile of soft, sweet-smelling clothes. It was so warm and cozy. The grandfather clock was gently ticking. Turnip closed his eyes. In a minute he was asleep.

BONG! BONG! BONG! The grandfather clock chimed the hour. Turnip sat bolt upright, wide awake and scared.

"Mama!" he howled. "MAMA!"

Mama and Papa raced down the stairs.

"Now, now," said Mama, hugging Turnip.

"Whatever are you doing down here in the laundry basket?" asked Papa.

"I had to find a bed without talkers, kickers, snorers, or grabbers," said Turnip.

"But this won't do," said Mama. "You can't sleep downstairs."

"That's right," said Papa. "Everyone sleeps in beds in bedrooms."

"Couldn't I sleep alone?" asked Turnip.

"All alone in your own bed?" asked Mama.

"Yes, please! In a bed of my very own."

"It's a fine idea," said Papa. "But we haven't got an extra bed."

"What about the laundry basket?" said Turnip.
"It would do," said Mama. "But not downstairs."

So Papa brought the basket up to a quiet corner of the kittens' bedroom. Mama made it up with sheets and blankets. Then Turnip climbed into his very own bed, and Mama and Papa kissed him good night.

Turnip snuggled under his covers, hugged his pillow, and fell fast and happily asleep.